*For David*

First published 2000 by Walker Books Ltd
87 Vauxhall Walk, London SE11 5HJ

2 4 6 8 10 9 7 5 3 1

© 2000 Kim Lewis

This book has been typeset in Goudy.

Printed in Hong Kong

British Library Cataloguing in Publication Data
A catalogue record for this book is available
from the British Library.

ISBN 0-7445-6731-9

# LITTLE PUPPY

## KIM LEWIS

WALKER BOOKS
AND SUBSIDIARIES
LONDON • BOSTON • SYDNEY

Today on Poppy's farm
a little puppy
opened its eyes.

The little puppy
looked at Poppy.
"Can I hold it,
Daddy?" Poppy said.

"Be gentle, Poppy,"
said Daddy.
"It's very little."

The little puppy squirmed and wriggled. Poppy softly stroked its fur.

The little puppy
licked Poppy's nose.
"I love you, little puppy,"
Poppy whispered.

"Let's put the puppy back with its mother," said Daddy.

Poppy tucked
the little puppy
next to its brothers
and sisters.

The little puppy closed
its eyes and fell asleep.

"See you tomorrow,
little puppy," said Poppy.